rhapsody 2018
an anthology of guelph writing

VP

Vocamus Press
Guelph, Ontario

Presented by Vocamus Writers Community

Published by Vocamus Press
©All rights reserved

Cover image of the Petrie Building
by David J. Knight, 2018
©All rights reserved

ISBN 13: 978-1-928171-73-7 (pbk)
ISBN 13: 978-1-928171-72-0 (ebk)

VP

Vocamus Press
130 Dublin Street, North
Guelph, Ontario, Canada
N1H 4N4

www.vocamus.net

2018

Preface

The Rhapsody Anthology is an annual collection of poetry presented by Vocamus Writers Community, a non-profit community organization that supports literary culture in Guelph, Ontario.

The anthology is a celebration of local writing that includes both authors who are well established in their craft and those who are published here for the first time, reflecting the writers and writing that formed the literary communities of Guelph during the year 2017/2018.

The cover art was provided by David J. Knight. The cover and interior were designed by Adam Dahari.

Acknowledgments

The Rhapsody Anthology is produced by Vocamus Writers Community, a non-profit community organisation that supports writing, publishing, and book culture in the Guelph area.

This season our work has been generously supported by Aaron Blair, June Blair, Nick Dinka, Kathryn Edgecombe, Alec Follett, Joy Goddard, Andrew Goodwin, Larry Harder, Arthur Hill, Paul Hock, Jaya James, Kathleen James, Michal Kleiza, Garth Laidlaw, Kim Lang, Jane Litchfield, Barbara & Bruce Matthews, Dan Pike, Greg Rhyno, Cheryl & Nicholas Ruddock, Bieke Stengos, Marian Thorpe, and Mark Whoachickie. We appreciate their support very much. If you'd also like to support the work of Friends of Vocamus Press, you can do so by searching us on www.patreon.com.

Thanks to all the contributors for sharing their work so generously. Special thanks to David J. Knight for allowing his art to be used for the book cover. Thanks finally to all those who contribute to the literary culture of Guelph as readers, writers, publishers, sponsors, venues, broadcasters, and in countless other ways – this collection is a celebration of all that you do.

rhapsody 2018
an anthology of guelph writing

CONTENTS

Remembering Colton   1
Nikki Everts

swift escape   3
Sheri Doyle

Sunkers   5
Nicholas Ruddock

Sojourn in Montreal   7
Sheila Koop

Digestive Disorders   9
Elaine Chang

Longing   11
Bieke Stengos

Silver-Sorrowed Clouds   13
Hanna Peters

My Plastic Childhood Christmas Knight 3   15
Jerry Prager

Al Purdy   17
Kathryn Edgecomb

Journey   19
Valerie Senyk

So Sadly Quietly Miss   21
Rob O'Flanagan

in les étoiles, i toil   23
jeffrey reid pettis

Benedictions 25
James Clarke

Hagiograph 27
Robin Elizabeth Downey

Neaped in Donegal 29
Michelle McMillan

What a Good Party It Might Have Been 31
Nora Ruddock

~~The~~ Salient ~~Unintended~~ 33
Darcy Hiltz

Likeness 35
Jeremy Luke Hill

Lice-pickin' Party 37
Marianne Micros

Insomnia 39
Kim Davids Mandar

Manitoba Street 41
Ann Clayton

Adolescence in Suburbia 43
Melinda Burns

Parvati 45
Andrea Perry

Denial Fog 47
Donna McCaw

Remembering Colton
Nikki Everts

Nikki Everts is a poet, author of mysteries, facilitator of writing workshops, provider of writing services through Scripted Images, willing performer, and a resident of Guelph. Her recently published connect dis connect, a chapbook of poetry published with the assistance of Vocamus Writers Community.

Remembering Colton

I stand on stolen ground
Blood calls faintly
Up through prairie grasses
Drums like heart beats
Mumbled messages thrumming

Who is our brother, oh settler?

I face east, south, west, north
Standing on stolen ground
Only a cloud of dust, small, distant
To the east, as of horses galloping
Or angels humming

Is this our brother, coming in clouds?

A car, a body, a gun, a man
A settler like me
Standing on stolen ground while
Life seeps out of some other mother's son
More blood drumming

Do you hear Rachel, weeping for her child?

An unrighteous king approved
The murder of sons, and today,
A boy is gone, chaff in the wind
His life's thief returns to stolen ground
To bloody messages mumbling

Where is our brother, oh settler?

A young brown man
No more foolish than our white ones
Is dead by our hand, and galloping
The dust, humming, is coming to answer
The blood calling from stolen ground

swift escape
Sheri Doyle

Sheri Doyle is a freelance writer and editor with over ten years of experience working in the publishing industry. She is the author of seven nonfiction books and numerous magazine and newspaper articles. As an editor, she has worked on book manuscripts, educational resources, and website content. Sheri also writes poetry and fiction.

Along with a BA (Hons) in Philosophy and English from York University, she has completed postgraduate courses in proofreading and editing from Simon Fraser University and Ryerson University.

swift escape

    she pulls the horizon close
    wraps herself in a cloak of setting sun

    don't look directly at her now, just imagine
    hydrogen, helium, and trace elements

    at 27 million degrees and swathed in
    nuclear fusion, she is cold at her core

    running through city streets after midnight
    a yellow flash on wet pavement

    ephemeral graffiti spotted only at safe angles
    she is blinding as a mechanism for swift escape

    a fire trail turning corners of buildings
    climbs lampposts for the warmth of dim bulbs

    sources tea lights behind foggy windows
    forever in search of a match to strike

    volatile gravity holding us together
    spinning tops in the solar flare

Sunkers
Nicholas Ruddock

Nicholas Ruddock is author of The Parabolist *(Doubleday 2010),* How Loveta Got Her Baby *(Breakwater 2014), and* Night Ambulance *(Breakwater 2016).*

Sunkers

I'm writing this
late at night when it's easy

no one remembers it but us

even the gibbous moon
which in that rare sky
blew down the path
and turned it into string
lit it up the way we felt
forgot it

so did the owl who turned away

something small and dark
swerved over
the wind-ripped black water
of Soldier's Pond

so high above the city
so high we were
the line of surf
laced all the way to Cappahayden
grass laid-out horizontal by
our breathing like that

no night for foghorns
everything plain as day
coast scarified
sunkers
shoals

count the wrecks.

Sojourn in Montreal
Sheila Koop

Sheila Koop is a writer who loves to filter landscape, experience and emotion through poetry. She also writes creative non-fiction short stories, and has dabbled in the romance genre of novel writing. Her poetry and short stories have won several awards from the Elora Writers Festival Competition. Sheila also co-edited an oral history of Wellington County, Older Voices Among Us. *The village of Elora is home turf to Sheila and she finds that its beautiful vistas of river and rock help to fuel the imagination. Apart from writing, Sheila is involved as a Board member of the Elora Centre for the Arts.*

Sojourn in Montreal

Crowds of three-storey apartments
with staircases that spiral through
the cold, ice and snow cascade
like children on toboggans close to
Mile End's no end of shopping and
and eating. Black-cloaked Hasidic
men with brilliant white stockings and
oversized hats that protect their space
on the narrow sidewalks beside the
hipsters in their overpriced second
hand sweaters and new Blundstone
boots. The fish mongers at Falerno's
feign boredom then proudly check each
oyster for freshness and I dream of
fish and seafood chowder until I happen
upon the perfect recipe, the one I always
use. How it will taste with fresh baguette
from Premiere Mossion where our daughter
spent a year behind the counters loaded
with buttery confections. Now she is the
mother who beckons me to dote upon
the princely Quinn. I acquiesce – remember
love passed on, as delicate and lovely
as snowflakes on an eyelash.

Digestive Disorders
Elaine Chang

Elaine Chang teaches critical theory, literatures and cultures of resistance, and creative writing at the University of Guelph.

Digestive Disorders

Mass expulsion can be habit forming,
a reflux reflex at corroded hinges.
Trachea and gullet, or drink and think
South: where hard ice fights insatiable thirst,
North: where one banana can cost five bucks.
It's no joke. Fresh fruit is very fragile.
Only sturdy exotics make the trek
and only when green, far from fit to eat.

A twin vermiculation, brain and gut,
splits these differences below the neck,
above the belt. Either way bass lines belch
hot sticky air, knot trope tricks. What we have
here is a failure to assimilate –
Choking coils, their walls punctured with ulcers.

Longing
Bieke Stengos

Bieke Stengos was born in Belgium, came to Canada as a young woman, and has lived here ever since, with time spent in various countries overseas. With that many places in her heart, she feels that she belongs to the world, and much of her work is set in Belgium and in Greece. She has published short stories and poetry in various journals, and has won several contests for her short stories.

Longing

Wish I too could bend
my course, on a calm sea
and reach without effort
where rays slant
to a distant horizon.

Wish I too could gather
stars, shimmering on the water
and reach without effort
what has been polished
by rougher waves.

Wish I too could sail
away, under heavenly clouds,
and reach without effort
my longed for
destination.

Silver-Sorrowed Clouds
Hanna Peters

Hanna Peters is a Zoology student studying at the University of Guelph. Having moved from the James Street South coffee shops of Hamilton, she brings one notebook with her everywhere until poems fill its pages. She is fueled by her passion for people, mental health awareness, playing French Horn and piano, cycling, science, her ferret, random sketches, and God's love.

Silver-Sorrowed Clouds

You misfortuned yourself
looking for black linings
on silver clouds
and passing them around.
You left yourself
at the door
today.
I can see it in your smile
dark enough
to turn your coffee black.

I hope the autumn
reminds you
that even leaves
know what it's like
to lose their colour

My Plastic Childhood Christmas Knight 3
Jerry Prager

Jerry Prager is the author of three volumes on the Calabrian mafia of Guelph, Legends of the Morgeti; *several books of poetry, is currently working on a series on fugitive slaves and how they came to Wellington County, the first and second of which books:* Laying the Bed: the Native Origins of the Underground Railroad, *and* Exodus and Arrival: Fugitive Roads to Guelph and Beyond *have already been published, The third book,* Blood in the Mortar: Freedom and Stone *is slated for publication in the spring of 2018. He is also preparing the first six books of a novel series.*

My Plastic Childhood Christmas Knight 3

Dust webs between his elbows and the haunch of his horse,
both rider and charger holding up well: the white stallion,
still legless and tail-less, proudly pretending
the page I moved them onto is a snow field
and that his legs are buried, its neck still defiantly aimed
where it was always fixed, but I've turned the knight's head
in its socket to face what the horse has been facing for years,
for decades, veering right since inception,
the knight usually gazing off to his left, or behind him,
until now, but the rooms and the views have changed
however many forgotten times since Christmas 1964,
the year my mother and father, sister and brother
came to my sickbed side, the year the knight and his horse
were given to cheer me.
My brother died two months ago
from self-inflicted liver failure; nine years before that,
my father died of self-inflicted lung disease,
my sister has been a common-law widow since June, my mother
is as defiant as the horse, and her legs only marginally better;
the knight, like me, is still cavalier in the saddle,
his gauntlet remains over his heart to hold his long-lost lance,
a hole for a hand that gapes like a chest wound.

Al Purdy
Kathryn Edgecombe

Kathryn Edgecombe has been able to indulge her love affair with words ever since she quit teaching and moved to the country. She now spends as much time as possible in her writing cabin by the pond. Her work has appeared in several journals and anthologies, and she has published three books of poetry, Not the First Waltz, Midwives to Our Selves, *and* Draw Me to the Flame.

Al Purdy

I'm no Al Purdy
but I've done battle
across the kitchen table
walls painted sunshine yellow
dishes organized on the shelves
according to size.

Conversation degenerating
to gaslight.
I fought for my life.

I'm a slow learner
repeating the same lessons
over and over.
A metaphorical gun shot,
a hole in my heart
light shone through.

Journey
Valerie Senyk

Valerie Senyk is a multi-media artist. She received her BFA and MA in Drama from the University of Saskatchewan, Saskatoon, and taught Theatre Arts at universities in Saskatchewan and Ontario for over 23 years. She is a playwright, an actor, and a published and recorded performance poet. She has published a full-length volume of poetry, I Want A Poem *(Vocamus Press, 2014). She is currently working on a chapbook of poetry and photography called* Stick.

Journey

    you saw the sky rip
    away from the horizon
    and the earth tip down

    you feared skidding
    into the coal mine of
    the universe

    spending your days flailing
    clouds blocking your view
    clouds eating your eyes

    these were just moments
    the uncounted ticks
    before the sky was stitched back
    into place

    they were necessary lessons in loss
    what else do you expect
    to be offered here as you voyage?

So Sadly Quietly Miss
Rob O'Flanagan

Rob O'Flanagan has been a newspaper reporter, photojournalist and columnist for nearly twenty years. He is the author of The Stories We Tell *and* The Blown Kiss Collection, *two volumes of short fiction. He writes, performs and records poetry, and is a visual artist. He lives in Guelph and is currently writing a novel.*

His collection of poetry, Open Up the Sky: A Poetic Conversation, *co-authored with Heather Cardin, is available from Vocamus Press.*

So Sadly Quietly Miss

I miss in so sadly
quietly a way
places that were
home and people
I have been
and companions now
flown or become someone
other than who
they were.

Love, this vapour I have
watched disperse so
sadly quietly rise and
vanish, vanish.

Some I loved I
still do so love
and some I loved
seem now so
disappeared.
And where?
Where?

I miss tonight my
camp on the island
where the bear gutted
my pack and left me
nothing but sardines
and raw vegetables.
I miss the trail where I
tempted the rattler
to strike my walking stick.
(The cries of campers
plunging from a cliff
across the bay).
With no companion
along with me
I so sadly
quietly missed my
old companions.

Sometimes when
I walk out along
the shores and high
up in the escarpment,
I pause to paw and gut
the air, sadly spilling,
sadly spilling all I so
sadly quietly miss.

in les étoiles, i toil
jeffrey reid pettis

jeffrey reid pettis studied English and Philosophy at Queen's University and now teaches high school within the Upper Grand District School board. He has published poems and short stories in various magazines and anthologies. jeffrey reid pettis listens to loud music loudly.

in les étoiles, i toil

if proportion is the measure of perfection,
i never was much good at drawing stars.
it was as if their crooked little limbs suffered
rigor mortis halfway through a jumping jack
or that they rehearsed stiff salutes to the sky,
then sank into shrugs, unable to be bothered
with decorum while also being relegated
into loose-leaf corners. but it's not like i
was light on practice; i doodled the divine
as eternity ticked away in long red seconds
in protest of the hour, and innumerable were
the shooting stars i claimed my own, shining
glibly with their symmetries uncoiled, bodies
frostbitten at the apex of their flights.

Benedictions
James Clarke

James Clarke is the author of almost twenty books of poetry and memoir, including Dreamworks, Forced Passage, How to Bribe a Judge, L'Arche Journal, A Mourner's Kaddish, The Raggedy Parade, Silver Mercies, *and* The Way Everyone is Inside. *He is a former Superior Court judge, and his judgments have been published extensively in legal journals. He lives in Guelph, Ontario.*

Benedictions

Sometimes when the world breaks over you
like a dark wave, distils the last small drop
of hope within your veins & baffled, you no
longer know where to turn or how to pray –

a sudden gift: bubbles of light on the ribbed
hull of a gold leaf along your way; a marsh
hawk, poised and imperious, white rump on
a pole in the belly of a bush, kee kee keeling into

the cool & colourless air; or on a bare fall night
furred with frost & just beyond your windowsill
a spill of stars, brilliant as the eyes of children,
earth's sweet-tongued orisons that nudge you

out of self, unlatch the chamber of your cold-
dumb heart, utter your own unspoken prayer.

Hagiograph
Robin Elizabeth Downey

Robin Elizabeth Downey was born under a much different name in Toronto, Ontario in 1952. She was a highschool teacher for many years, using her summers to roadtrip across North America, sometimes as far south as Costa Rica. She was bisexual long before most people knew exactly what that meant. She never married but has two adult children.

She now makes her home in Guelph, Ontario.

Hagiograph

Will you grant me
a bright halo
for miracles
performed by my
tongue between your
thighs
        When I die
just a little
will you unbind
my winding sheets
to reveal me
still naked and
incorrupt
        Will
you cut relics
from my hair and
wear them sacred
about your neck
to feel your prayers
like the kisses

Neaped in Donegal
Michelle McMillan

Former Assistant-Director of Guelph Museums and Owner of Ki Design, Michelle McMillan is now retired and doing what she loves most – writing and gardening. She has studied writing with Melinda Burns, Lorraine Gane, Brian Henry and the International Writing Program of the University of Iowa. From 2003 to 2012 she published TongRen, *the quarterly journal of the Canadian Taiijquan Federation. Her poems and essays have been published in* Rhapsody; Guelph Speaks; TongRen; *and* Vox feminarum. *She has written a privately commissioned biography and is presently working on a literary memoir..*

Neaped in Donegal

The Gueabarra River
runs black with peat,
spawns silver flashes,
breathes molten pewter,
flows lustrous to the moon.

She withdraws with the dark
as dawn's languid light
casts pale gold
into her shadow;
reveals a wanton disposition.

Embedded with archaic gems,
she is adorned in
milk of magnesia blue,
poison green and
whiskey opalescence.

An anchor hangs from a chain.
Rills mount iron pots,
horseshoes and steel cables
into the stiff prongs
of sheep ribs and thigh bones.

The river remembers
womenfolk in plaid wool skirts,
shepherds, blacksmiths,
drunken poets and sailors –
stonesetters all, there as the tide serves.

I am a blow-in from
a parallel universe,
neaped in Donegal,
enamoured by the rising and falling

What a Good Party It Might Have Been
Nora Ruddock

Nora Ruddock is a poet living in Guelph. Her work has appeared in magazines like the Antigonish Review *and in art installations like* Inner Arts Matrix *and* Tinderbox.

What a Good Party It Might Have Been

That day you were sitting in the horse-drawn sled opening a parcel of cakes and fruit and books sent by a friend, hard snow falling all around. "Wind like an axe," you said. She dropped the tangerines. The sled had to stop, you gave the tangerines to the children and how orange they looked against the snow, against the dark evergreens crowding close. It was hard to believe in the festivities. You said you saw yourself wearing a backpack and walking away, getting the hell out. And eventually it was so, you got away and she wore the yellow silk slip and the red jacket, with that brooch of ivory that made you so uneasy.

Up north we brought all the clothes we stopped wearing during the year. I found treasures, jeans that fit better than my current ones, summer dresses, faded, soft, to wear when the sun was hot, to feel the wind. She in a cotton shift, magenta, moving through the forest to her studio. An empty nest that morning, perfect, small, needles woven round and round. She brought it with her to look at the shape, at the scoop of space, the round, full, sorrowful cup. Birds all fledged, songs tentative in the dawn, the air surrounding, questioning. A falcon cried on down the channel, but far enough, that day, to shoulder against the wind.

~~The~~ Salient ~~Unintended~~
Darcy Hiltz

Darcy R. Hiltz grew up in Nova Scotia and moved to Guelph in 2004. He holds a BA Honours in History and Sociology from Acadia University, a MLIS from Dalhousie University, and a Certificate of Creative Writing from Conestoga College. Darcy is an Archivist / Librarian at Guelph Public Library, an amateur genealogist after being exposed to family history through a 4-H project, and an experienced farm hand. He has published a chapbook of poetry called Beyond All This *(Fenylalanine Publishing, 2015).*

~~The~~ Salient ~~Unintended~~

    masking tape
    strips horizontal horizontally
    across a library washroom door
    some broken
    hang silent hung? Dangle
    like the universal man
    on blue sign
    with temporary
    stuck on
    white laminate
    out of order sign
    below

    I read

            Men
            Out of Order

Likeness
Jeremy Luke Hill

Jeremy Luke Hill is the publisher at Vocamus Press, a micro-press that publishes the literary culture of Guelph, Ontario. He is also the Managing Director at Friends of Vocamus Press, a non-profit community organization that supports book culture in Guelph.

He has written a collection of poetry, short prose and photography called Island Pieces, *a chapbook of poetry called* These My Streets, *and an ongoing series of poetry broadsheets called* Conversations with Viral Media. *His criticism and poetry have appeared in places like* The Bull Calf, CV2, EVENT Magazine, Free Fall, The Goose, paperplates, Queen Mob's Tea House, The Rusty Toque, The Town Crier, *and* The Windsor Review.

Likeness

I'm afraid of our likeness, son,
that we are both of us too quick
to face God down in his absence,
tell him – "Fuck you, man! You're not my
real dad. Not my real mom either." –
await whatever lightening won't
alight from that too patient or
disinterested divinity.

We neither of us learned to become
as little children, because – "God!
What the hell good was it to be
child-like among men?" – so we spoke,
and we reasoned, as mannish boys,
bit the teat, mouthed the meal, spat it
back on the plate, could never ask –
"Am I your son? Are you well-pleased?"

Lice-pickin' Party
Marianne Micros

Marianne Micros was an Associate Professor at the University of Guelph, teaching literature and creative writing. She is the author of the poetry collections, Upstairs Over the Ice Cream *(Ergo Productions, 1979),* Seventeen Trees *(Guernica Editions, 2007), and* The Key of Dee.

Lice-pickin' Party

gathered together in someone's house or maybe a town hall
mothers and children and a few fathers   the children and
maybe some adults have to wash their hair with special shampoo
before they come   they are asked at the door if they did so
then the parents pick lice out of their children's hair with special combs
they yell egg whenever they find one and groan when they find
a live louse hey come look at this one   or can you help me is this
an egg or not?   the richer people are uppity   they look down on
the waitress who is a single mom never married   maybe she caused
this infestation   lice prefer clean hair she says   guessing their
thoughts   a potluck supper is spread out on a table in the next
room   away from those ugly bugs   occasionally someone washes
her hands and has a carrot, a cracker with cheddar cheese, or
a chocolate chip cookie   the children want to run and play but
are forced to sit while their heads are examined and picked at

once released children dash outside or head for the rec room
some of them watch a movie on tv or play video games
don't put anyone else's hat on   don't touch the waitress's son
mothers whisper to their children   they flirt with the single dad
offer chocolate brownies to the grandfather who is raising
a rebellious teen

they pretend they never came here   never had to clean out
the sordid creatures from young heads and their own brains

never tell   say this is a potluck supper   everything now is clean
as sterile as a newborn baby   children can play now

until the next outbreak creeps in   the monsters leap from
head to head   polluting sheets and towels and sofas
keeping children home from school   forcing adults to meet
in this place of dirty secrets

tonight the adults will dream of things crawling in their heads
through every hair

tomorrow oblivious children will play
hug each other   wrestle   touch   run   scratch their heads
when adults are not looking   swap hats gleefully

Insomnia
Kim Davids Mandar

As a student in the Creative Writing program at The University of Guelph, Kim continues to explore poetry, fiction and creative nonfiction as her favourite media. Kim's first children's book about global migration — There is Beauty Here Because You Are Here — has been a fabulous collaboration with local artist Alura Sutherland, and the workshopping and publishing process is moving apace. Professional writing continues in her work as Content Co-ordinator for Best Version Media's local magazine Neighbours of South End Guelph. *Kim instructs at The Conestoga Language Institute — Conestoga College, in Kitchener.*

Insomnia

Rattling day's end, hunting sleep in the dark
mind splintered through moments past and near.
Vigilant currents, stupor in the stark
cold ramblings — possibility unclear.
And now, victimless prey of the night
floating, adrift in a mirage of time,
cunning oasis of suspended flight
wakened by daylight's destined climb.
Into this patterned trap we fall
scarce scattered by the consequence;
heedless of our wisdom's call
to ward off the bitter insolence.
As deprivation wears us thin,
No insight nor triumph find we therein.

Manitoba Street
Ann Clayton

Ann Clayton was a teacher of Commonwealth literature at the University of Guelph and the University of Waterloo. She was a teacher of literature at universities in Johannnesburg, South Africa, where she also worked as a writer, free lance journalist and book reviewer.

She has published several book-length academic titles, as well as three previous volumes of poetry.

Manitoba Street

The world began to speak
to me in many tongues
and songs rang through stone,
flowered in music, calling
through all creatures, home.

The spirit began to write
in features and faces,
language making them one,
the world their monumental book
of difference, uttered as bone.

Time became a rope I climbed,
twisting memory and hope,
a scroll disclosing future and past
as I scribbled in the fury of now,
each moment a magic lantern, held fast.

Being reeled out its mystery
of change and self, calling itself
forward, a fisherman's shining line
cast into water, a thread into
darkness, a lamp in the mine.

Love opened a family album
of photographs, greetings, cards.
The world collected in Lost and Found
of gloves, coats, pictures and words.
Blessings descended in this place: new
ground.

Adolescence in Suburbia
Melinda Burns

Melinda Burns is a writer and a psychotherapist in private practice in Guelph, Ontario, where she also teaches writing. Her writing has won awards for fiction, including first prize in the Toronto Star Short Story contest in 2001 and first prize in the Elora Writers' Festival Writing Contest in 2008. She has published poems in various magazines, read her essays on CBC radio, and published essays on writing in Canadian Notes and Queries *and in K.D. Miller's book on creativity and spirituality,* Holy Writ. *Melinda lives in Guelph, Ontario, within walking distance of the public library.*

Adolescence in Suburbia

This is a poem for you
in your unhatched egg
your suburban quarantine
trapped in amber
aimless time
waiting out your teenage sentence

walking to the mall
to buy the frosted pink
lipstick you thought
might make the transformation
glasses in your pocket
preferring to squint

nothing to see but
look-alike houses and
rivers of cars
Poking at your hair
in the bathroom mirror
after tossing all night

on prickly brush rollers
and still
it goes up when you
want it to go down
and down
when you want it to go up

Parvati
Andrea Perry

Andrea Perry graduated from the Royal Military College of Canada in 2008 with a BA in English Literature and a Minor in Political Science. She served five years as an Intelligence Officer in the Canadian Army before releasing in 2013 to pursue a life-times long, multi-dimensional love of reading and writing. She has since completed an MFA in Creative Writing at the University of Guelph and now drifts between hometown Ottawa, new-town Guelph, and other travels. She writes poetry and fiction. Her debut collection of poetry, Rise, *was published by Vocamus Press in 2016.*

Parvati

Meditations, lately, have been full
of Shiva

Streaming blue, height of the Himalayas
He kneels

earth-sized face in mine, 3rd eye
opens a blissful destruction

You don't need any of this, I hear
and disintegrate

attachments disband in a surprise
wind

The snake uncoils
at His collar

When I open my eyes, my face
in the mirror is as large as His

We smile
In each of our thousand arms

solar systems topple
on their axes

Denial Fog
Donna McCaw

Donna McCaw has written five books: Sing a Song of Six Packs, *which claims to remember the 1960's;* Spiral to the Heart *and* The Spell of Crazy Love, *which are both poetry collections;* Under the Apple Boughs, *shorts stories about rural living in Ontario and Saskatchewan; and* It's Your Time, *a recently updated nonfiction title about getting ready for retirement. She organizes Wordfest in April and October at the Elora Centre for the Arts, and does storytelling at various venues.*

Denial Fog

Pillowed, unaware of water thieves,
Baby killers, woman butchers,
Big black dogs
Playing golf with those greasy bones.

Smiling, hat tipping,
Safe sleeping in sterile beds
As the heat creeps up
Backyard burger flipping
Over The Fire the Next Time.

Cashing cheques, eating peaches,
Swiping plastic for Botox dreams of youth
Cutting pesticide laced lawns
All pawns, the king's castled and gone
Where fish bones and plastic bags cover beaches.

Buy Buy Buy the advertising cry
Images of model's skeletal bodies, make-up masks
Bloody diamonds for fairy tale weddings
Quicksand debt holes, slavery roles
Quell the fear, play the game.

In a fog of their own
In a box house in town
Built where the trees were cut down
To make another sub standard division
This safe vision subject to sudden revision.

Pompeii ignoring the tremors
Senators lounging at their baths
Preserved in magma and dust
In their magnificent resorts
No one believed such strange reports.

Water slowly cooking frogs
In stupidity soup and denial fog.

Vocamus Writers Community

Vocamus Writers Community is a non-profit community organisation that supports book culture in Guelph and the surrounding area. It runs workshops, writing groups, and writer hang-outs. It offers resources for writers looking to publish their work both traditionally and independently. It promotes readings, launches, and other literary events in the community. It also produces the annual *Rhapsody* anthology. For more information, email info@vocamus.net.